PAPAGAYO

The Mischief Maker

PAPA

Voyager Books
Harcourt, Inc.

San Diego   New York   London

GAYO

The Mischief Maker

Written and illustrated by

Gerald McDermott

First published by Windmill Books Inc., and
Wanderer Books, a Simon & Schuster imprint.

Voyager Books is a registered
trademark of Harcourt, Inc.

Library of Congress Cataloging-in-Publication Data
McDermott, Gerald.
Papagayo the mischief maker/written and illustrated
by Geral McDermott.
p.   cm.
Summary: Papagayo, the noisy parrot, helps the night animals
save the moon from being eaten up by the moon-dog.
ISBN 0-15-259465-5
ISBN 0-15-259464-7 (pbk.)
[1. Parrots — Fiction. 2. Jungles — Fiction.] I. Title.
PZ7.M4784173Pap   1992
[E] — dc20   91-40364

M L K J I H G F E D
Q P O N M L K J   (pbk.)

The illustrations in this book were
done in gouache and colored pencils.
The display and text type were set in Benguiat.
Color separations were made by Bright Arts, Ltd., Singapore.
Printed and bound by Tien Wah Press, Singapore.
Production supervision by Warren Wallerstein and Diana Novak.
Typography designed by Camilla Filancia.

Printed in Singapore

For Jane, Jack, and Alice

Papagayo woke up with the sun. He ruffled his bright feathers and opened wide his yellow beak and greeted the morning with a raucous *"Crawk! Cara-cara-cao-cao-cao!"* The night creatures were fast asleep. But Papagayo was awake and he made mischief.

Sometimes he would steal fruit from the spider monkey.

Sometimes he would surprise the butterflies and send them fluttering in every direction.

Sometimes he would fly high up in the sky clutching a big nut, then drop it with a "*crak!*" on the armadillo's shell.

Whatever Papagayo was up to, he always made a lot of noise. This disturbed the sleep of the night creatures. They would wake up and say, "Please be quiet, Papagayo." The parrot would not stop squawking, and then they would complain, "Not so loud, Papagayo." But the parrot still wouldn't stop. Finally the night creatures would get angry and scream, "Papagayo, shut your beak!"

At night, while Papagayo slept, the night creatures would venture forth in the moonlight. They would gaze at the white sugar-moon and croon quiet songs all night long. As dawn approached, they would settle down to sleep through the hot jungle day.

No sooner had the night creatures closed their eyes than Papagayo was up, looking for fresh fruit and fresh mischief.

One morning, Papagayo was especially loud. The sleepy-eyed sloth had a talk with the bird.

"Papagayo," said the sloth, "you make entirely too much noise. You disturb the peaceful sleep of the night creatures."

"*Crawk!* Sleepyheads! Why don't you laugh and play all day as I do?" asked the parrot.

"The day is too bright and full of sounds. It makes us afraid, so we hide from the sunlight and the noise. But at night we can creep out beneath the moonbeams and sing gentle songs. We sing softly, because we are afraid to disturb the quiet of the night."

"Afraid? Afraid!" clucked Papagayo. "How can you ever be happy if you are always afraid? Ridiculous!" Papagayo ruffled his feathers, twirled around the branch, and flew away over the treetops.

When darkness fell, the creatures of the night gathered as usual to gaze lovingly at the moon. They looked up with watchful eyes and made soft moon music.

Many miles away, in the heart of the rain forest, something stirred beneath the stones of the Great Ruined City. It was the ghost of an ancient monster dog awakening from a deep sleep. He was a moon eater, and when he woke up, he was very, very hungry. He saw the moon—round, sweet, and delicious—hanging in the sky, and he licked his lips.

The bony moon-dog slipped from the ruins and floated up into the sky. He loped along the pathway of the stars toward the moon.

All the night creatures gasped when they saw the fierce moon-dog pounce on the moon. They watched in terrified silence as he began to nibble at it. Then the moon-dog took a big bite out of the moon, scurried across the starry fields of the sky, and disappeared within the crumbling walls of the Great Ruined City.

The next night, the creatures of the rain forest gathered under the stars. Trembling, they looked up at the bite-sized shape that was missing from the moon.

"Perhaps the moon-dog won't come anymore. Perhaps he is satisfied," they whispered. "We can't complain if just a tiny bit of the moon is missing. Perhaps our beloved moon will grow again and be full."

But at midnight the moon-dog came again. He bared his sharp teeth and hungrily began to eat the moon. To the horror of the forest creatures, he returned each night for a week. As the moon-dog grew fatter and fatter, the moon became thinner and thinner.

After seven nights, the creatures of the rain forest were too frightened to sleep. They sat silent, blinking in the unfamiliar sunlight, red-eyed and sad, not knowing what to do.

Papagayo came flying along just then, singing and chuckling to himself. He was surprised to find all the night creatures wide awake.

"*Crawk!* Good morning, my bleary-eyed friends." Papagayo laughed. "Isn't it past your bedtime?"

"It's not funny, Papagayo," they said, pouting. "It's terrible! Each night this week a moon-dog has eaten a bit of our beloved moon. There is only the thinnest sliver left. Tonight he's sure to swallow the last of it, and night will be nothing more than everlasting darkness."

"Disgusting!" spat Papagayo. "Why don't you stop him?"

"Because we're afraid," the night creatures answered in chorus. "There's nothing we can do."

"Nothing? Nothing! *Craaawk!* There is always something one can do. I'll stay up with you tonight, my friends, and we shall see what is to be done."

That night, Papagayo kept a vigil with the night creatures. It was very dark, because the moon was now just a slender crescent, but Papagayo tried hard to stay awake. He was just about to doze off when he heard the creatures whimpering.

The moon-dog had returned and he was bigger and fatter than ever. He greedily licked the last sweet bit of the moon.

"Oh, what shall we do?" the night creatures moaned. "He is eating the last of it! What shall we do?"

Papagayo jumped up. "Make noise!" he shouted. "You must make noise." The parrot flew to a high branch and began to screech, "*Craaaaaawk! Cara-cao-cao-cao!*"

At Papagayo's call, the night creatures began to stir. At first they were timid, but gradually they began to yell and shout. Their sounds grew louder and louder until the jungle echoed with their cries. They howled and hissed and croaked. They cracked sticks and shook bushes and beat a rhythm that every night creature joined in chanting: *"Chaca-chaca-chaca-chaca-chaca-chaca,"* and Papagayo shouted, *"Cao-cao-cao!"*

The moon-dog was frightened by all the noise. He jumped off the moon and ran through the sky. He fled along the pathway of the stars and disappeared into the darkness of the Great Ruined City.

"We did it!" shouted the night creatures. "We scared away the moon eater. How brave we are! Now our beloved moon can grow again to fullness."

Papagayo cocked his head and clucked, "Now that the moon-dog has tasted the sweetness of the moon, he is sure to sneak back. When he comes again, remember what you must do."

But the night creatures, proud of their great victory, and tired from all the excitement, were already curling up for a good day's sleep.

The sun began to color the sky. Papagayo ruffled his feathers and spread his wings. He opened his yellow beak and greeted the morning with a loud and raucous *"Crawk! Cara-cara-cao-cao-cao!"*

Not a single creature complained.

Also by Gerald McDermott

C O Y O T E

A Trickster Tale from the American Southwest

R A V E N

A Trickster Tale from the Pacific Northwest

Z O M O   T H E   R A B B I T

A Trickster Tale from West Africa